By Melissa Lagonegro
Illustrated by Elisa Marrucchi

A Random House PICTUREBACK® Book
Random House 🏠 New York

ISBN: 978-0-7364-2453-0   Library of Congress Control Number: 2006928027

www.randomhouse.com/kids/disney

Printed in the United States of America   35 34 33 32 31 30 29 28   First Edition

A princess loves to celebrate Halloween. It's the perfect time of year to plan a sweet and spooky party with friends!

Cinderella carves big orange pumpkins. Gus and Jaq love to help!

When Cinderella finishes carving, she turns the pumpkins into glowing jack-o'-lanterns.

Flora, Fauna, and Merryweather love using magic
to create colorful costumes for Princess Aurora.

Ariel uses seashells and seaweed to make silly masks for the Halloween Festival under the sea. *Arrrrrh!* Flounder is a pirate!

Belle bakes sweet Halloween treats for the Beast.
Pumpkin pie is his favorite!

Cinderella hands out candy to all the trick-or-treaters who come to the castle. Gus likes to fill a little candy bag of his own!

The Dwarfs love bobbing for apples. Dopey is the best.
He doesn't have a beard to get in the way!

Halloween is a time for tricks. In their silly and creepy costumes, Ariel and Flounder surprise Sebastian and say . . . BOO!

It is also a time for treats. Snow White stuffs bags of sweets for all the Dwarfs.

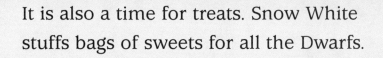

Halloween can also be a spooky time—especially in the Beast's castle! Belle tells scary Halloween stories that make even the Beast tremble with fright.

With fish and merfolk wearing creepy costumes, even the sea can seem very spooky on Halloween. Flounder is scared to swim through the dark caves and grottoes.

But Halloween is also a time for fun! With a little magic, Cinderella and the Prince ride in a carriage that really *is* a giant pumpkin!

Costumes and carvings, candy and cobwebs, tricks and treats—
Halloween is surely the sweetest and spookiest time of all!

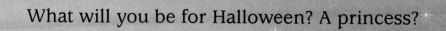

What will you be for Halloween? A princess?